Thomas' Story Collection

The Rev. W. Awdry
Illustrated by Robin Davies

Thomas and James

The Rev. W. Awdry
Illustrated by Robin Davies

Every morning The Fat Controller came to the station to catch his train. He always said "Hello" to Thomas the Tank Engine. Thomas worked hard every day pushing and pulling all the trucks into the right places.
"I need to learn all about the trucks to become a Really Useful Engine," Thomas told himself.

There were some funny-looking trucks in a siding. There was a small coach, some flat trucks, and a strange thing that his Driver called a crane.

"That's the breakdown train," said the Driver. "When there is an accident, the engine takes the workmen to clear and mend the line. The crane is for lifting heavy things, like engines, coaches and trucks."

One day, Thomas was in the Yard, when he heard an engine whistling "Help! Help!" A goods train came rushing through much too quickly.

The engine was a new engine called James and he was very frightened. His brake blocks were on fire, and flames and sparks were streaming out on each side.
"They're pushing me! They're pushing me!" panted James.

"On! On! On! On!" laughed the trucks, pushing James along the rails. "Help! Help!" whistled James as he disappeared out of sight.

"I hope James will be all right," thought Thomas, but it was already too late. The trucks pushed James right off the rails!

Suddenly a bell rang in the signal box and a man came running down the Yard towards Thomas.
"James is off the line – we must get the breakdown train – quickly!" shouted the man.

Thomas was coupled on, the workmen jumped into the coach and off they went as fast as they could.
"Hurry! Hurry! Hurry!" puffed Thomas, working as hard as he could.

They found James and the trucks on a bend in the line.
The brake van and the last few trucks were still on the rails,
but the front ones were piled in a heap next to James.

Poor James was looking very unhappy.
"I'd like to teach those trucks a lesson," thought Thomas.

James' Driver and Fireman were feeling him
all over to see if he was hurt.
"Never mind, James," said the Fireman.
"It wasn't your fault," said the Driver. "It was those
wooden brakes. We always said they were no good."

Thomas used the breakdown train to pull the unhurt trucks out of the way. He worked hard all afternoon, pulling all the other trucks back to the Yard as well.

"This'll teach you a lesson! This'll teach you a lesson!"
Thomas told the trucks.
"Yes it will, yes it will," they said in sad, creaky voices.

The workmen mended the line and then lifted James back onto the rails with the crane.
"Steady!" said one of the workmen, as they lifted James into the air.
"Carefully now," said another, as they put James back on to the rails.
"Oh dear, I can't move!" said James.

Thomas took James back to the engine shed to be mended.
The Fat Controller was waiting for them, anxiously.
"I'm very pleased with you, Thomas," said The Fat Controller.

"You're a Really Useful Engine. We'll give James some new brakes and a shiny new coat of paint, and Thomas – you shall have a branch line all to yourself."
"Oh, thank you, Sir!" said Thomas, happily.

Thomas was very happy to have his very own branch line. He puffed proudly backwards and forwards with two coaches every day.

Best of all, Thomas liked picking up all the passengers at the stations and taking them on their journey.

Thomas often saw the other engines at the junctions. Some of them stopped to say hello, and some, like Gordon, didn't have time to stop, but said "Poop, poop!" as they rushed past.

And Thomas always whistled "Peep, peep!" in return.

Thomas Comes
to Breakfast

The Rev. W. Awdry
Illustrated by Robin Davies

Dedicated to the memory of
Stuart James Eggenton (1992-96),
a little boy who loved to have his breakfast with Thomas.

Thomas the Tank Engine has worked his branch line for many years. "You know just when to stop," laughed his Driver one day. "You could almost manage without me."

Thomas didn't understand that his Driver was only joking.
"Driver says that I don't need him anymore," he told the others.

"Don't be so silly," said Percy.
"I'd never go without my Driver,"
said Toby earnestly. "I'd be frightened."

"Pooh!" boasted Thomas. "I'm not scared. Just you wait and see."

It was dark in the morning when the Firelighter came to light the engines. Thomas drowsed comfortably as the warmth spread through his boiler.

He woke again in daylight. Percy and
Toby were still asleep.
"I'll give those silly stick-in-the-muds
a surprise," he chuckled.

He felt steam going into one piston, and then to the other.
"I'm moving! I'm moving!" he whispered. "I'll creep outside
and stop. Then I'll wheesh loudly to make them jump."

Thomas thought he was clever, but really he was only moving because a careless cleaner had meddled with his controls. He tried to wheesh, but he couldn't. He tried to stop, but he couldn't. He just kept rolling along.

"Never mind, the buffers will stop me," he thought hopefully.

But that siding had no buffers. The rails ended at the road. Thomas' wheels left the rails and crunched the tarmac. Ahead of him was a hedge, a garden gate and the Stationmaster's house.

The Stationmaster and his family were having breakfast. It was
their favourite one of bacon and eggs.
"Oh horrors!" exclaimed Thomas as he shut his eyes and plunged
through the hedge.

There was a crash, the house rocked, plaster peppered the plates. Thomas peered through the broken window. He couldn't speak.

The Stationmaster strode outside. He shut off the steam and surveyed his wrecked garden.

His wife picked up the plates. "You miserable engine," she scolded, "just look at our breakfast – covered in plaster. Now I shall have to cook some more." She banged the door behind her.

They finished their breakfast in the kitchen and left Thomas sulking
on his own. More and more plaster fell. Thomas wanted to sneeze,
but he didn't dare in case the house fell on top of him.

No one came near him for a very long time – everyone was much too busy. At last some workmen arrived to prop the house up with strong poles.

Next they brought a load of sleepers and made a road over the garden so that Donald and Douglas, puffing hard, could pull Thomas back to the rails again.

Thomas looked so comic that the twins laughed aloud.
"Goodbye Thomas," they chuckled. "Don't forget your Driver next
time!" His Driver and Fireman began to tidy him up. "You're a
perfect disgrace," they told him. "We're ashamed of you."

"And so am I," said a voice behind them. "You're a very
naughty engine," The Fat Controller continued.
"Yes, Sir, I'm sorry, Sir," faltered Thomas.

"You must go to the Works to be mended, but they've no time for you now. Percy will take you to a siding where you can wait till they are ready."

Next day a diesel railcar came.
"That's Daisy," said the Fat Contoller. "She's come to do your
work. Diesels never run off to breakfast in Stationmasters' houses."
And he walked sternly away.

Thomas didn't enjoy his time at the Works. "It's nice to feel mended again," he said afterwards, "but they took so many of my old parts away and put new ones in, that I'm not sure whether I'm really me or another engine."

When Thomas came home, he soon made friends with Daisy.
In fact, Thomas is glad to have her help with his passengers.
He is now never so silly as to think he can manage without
his Driver.

Thomas and Gordon off the Rails

The Rev. W. Awdry
Illustrated by Robin Davies

"Wake up, Gordon," said his Driver one morning. "You've got a special train to pull, today."

"Is it coaches or trucks?" asked Gordon.

"Trucks," said his Driver.

"Trucks!" grumbled Gordon. "I won't go. I won't go!"
Gordon began to sulk and his fire wouldn't burn properly.
When Edward pushed him to the turntable, he didn't help at all.

Gordon hissed loudly. "Trucks! I'll show them." And when the
turntable was half-way round, he moved slowly forward. He only
meant to go far enough to jam the turntable, but once he was
moving forward he found he couldn't stop.

"Whoosh," he said as he went right off the rails, slithered down a bank and landed in a ditch.

The Yard Manager was very cross. "Look what you've done, you silly great engine!" he bellowed. "It will be hours before we can get you out of here."

"Glug," said Gordon, apologetically.

It was dark when the breakdown gang came for Gordon. They brought floodlights and powerful jacks. A crane lifted Gordon's tender clear and then the workmen attached strong cables to the back of his cab.

Then the men built a ramp of sleepers and James and Henry, pulling hard, managed to get Gordon back on to the rails. "Not such a splendid engine now, are you?" teased a workman. It was true. Gordon was very wet, very dirty, and he smelt awful!

A few days later, Thomas was at the junction when Gordon arrived with some trucks.
"Pooh!" remarked Thomas to Annie and Clarabel. "Can you smell a smell? A funny, musty sort of smell?"

"No," said Annie and Clarabel. "We can't smell a smell."
"Do you know what I think it is?" said Thomas, staring at Gordon.
"It's ditch water!" But before Gordon could answer, Thomas had
quietly puffed away, giggling to himself.

Later, Thomas took some empty trucks to a mine. Long ago, miners digging for lead had tunnelled into the ground. One of the tunnels went right under the railway line and the ground above was weak.

At a fork in the sidings, a large notice board said, "DANGER. Engines Must Not Pass This Point." Thomas had often tried to get past, but he had never succeeded. Today, though, he had a plan. As his Fireman got out to change the points, Thomas' Driver leaned out of the cab to see where he was going.

"Now!" said Thomas to himself and, bumping the trucks fiercely, he jerked the Driver off the footplate. "Stupid old board, there's no danger," he said as he followed the trucks past the board. There was a loud rumbling sound and the ground in front of Thomas started to cave in.

"Look out!" shouted Thomas' Driver. The Fireman scrambled into the cab and put Thomas' brakes on. But it was too late. "Fire and smoke!" shouted Thomas, "I'm sinking." And he was. The rails broke and he slid into the pit below.

"Oh dear," Thomas said. "I am a silly engine."
"And a very naughty one, too," said a familiar voice behind him.
"Please get me out, Sir," said Thomas. "I won't be naughty again."
"I'm not so sure," said The Fat Controller. "We can't lift you out
with a crane. The ground isn't firm enough. We might have to leave
you there for sometime . . ."
"Leave me . . . here?" wailed Thomas.

The Fat Controller thought for a while. "Hmmn," he said,
"I wonder if Gordon could pull you out."
Thomas stumbled out a reply, "G . . . G . . . Gordon?" He wasn't
sure he wanted to see Gordon again just yet.

When Gordon heard about Thomas' accident, he laughed loudly. "Down a mine is he?" he asked James and Edward. "How fitting – I always said that he was a minor engine. Ho-Ho-Ho!" But he hurried to the rescue all the same.

Gordon reached the mine and carefully drew up behind Thomas.
"Poop-poop, little Thomas, have you got that sinking feeling?" he whistled. "We'll have you out of there in a couple of puffs."

Workmen fastened strong cables between the two engines. "Are you ready?" called The Fat Controller. "One, two, three, HEAVE." Very slowly and very carefully, Gordon pulled Thomas back on the rails to safety.

"Thank you for rescuing me," said Thomas to Gordon, "I was in a bit of a hole!"
His Driver and Fireman checked him over to see where he was hurt. "I'm sorry I was cheeky," said Thomas.

"That's all right, Thomas," said Gordon. "You made me laugh.
I like that."
Then he whispered carefully, "I'm in disgrace, you know, and it
cheered me up."

Gordon started to tow Thomas back towards Tidmouth.
"I'm in disgrace, too," said Thomas as they started their journey.
"Why so you are, Thomas," Gordon replied. "We're both in
disgrace. Shall we form an alliance?"
"An ally – what?" asked Thomas.
"An alliance, Thomas. United we stand, together we fall," said
Gordon grandly. "You help me and I'll help you."

"Right you are," said Thomas.
"Good! That's settled, then," rumbled Gordon.
And buffer to buffer the allies puffed home.